D1257771

Weekly Reader Children's Book Club presents

The Baby Beebee Bird

STORY AND PICTURES BY

Diane Redfield Massie

HARPER & ROW, PUBLISHERS · NEW YORK, EVANSTON, AND LONDON

This book is a presentation of
Weekly Reader Children's Book Club.

Weekly Reader Children's Book Club
offers book clubs for children from
preschool through junior high school.
All quality hardcover books are selected by
a distinguished Weekly Reader Selection board.

For further information write to:
Weekly Reader Children's Book Club
1250 Fairwood Ave.
Columbus, Ohio 43216

for Nu Nu

The animals at the zoo had roared and growled and hissed and meowed all day long.
They were very tired.

"It's eight o'clock," yawned the elephant,
and he settled down in his big hay bed.
"I've eaten 562 peanuts today," he said,
but no one heard him. They were all asleep.

The zoo was very still.........until....

"beebeebobbibobbi beebeebobbibobbi beebeebobbibobbi beebeebobbibobbi..."

"What," said the elephant, "is that?"
"It's the baby beebee bird," said the giraffe.
"He's new to the zoo."

"Well, tell him to be quiet,"
growled the leopard.
"I want to sleep."

"beebeebobbibobbi beebeebobbibobbi beebeebobbibobbi beebeebobbibobbi..."

"Be quiet, please," said the giraffe politely.
"But I can't," said the beebee bird.
"I'm wide awake.
beebeebobbibobbi beebeebobbibobbi beebeebobbibobbi beebeebobbibobbi . . ."

"Quiet!" roared the lion.

"He's wide awake," explained the giraffe.

"Why isn't he tired like the rest of us?" growled the bear.

"Aren't you tired?" asked the giraffe.

"No," said the beebee bird.

"I've slept all the day and now it's time for me to sing. . . .

beebeebobbibobbi beebeebobbibobbi beebeebobbibobbi beebeebobbibobbi . . ."

"Oh, dear," said the elephant,
"and I am so sleepy."

"beebeebobbibobbi beebeebobbibobbi beebeebobbibobbi . . ."

"QUIET!!!" shouted all the animals. "WE CAN'T SLEEP!!!"

beebeebobbi

"beebeebobbibobbi

beebeebobbi

beebeebobbibobbi

beebeebobbi

beebeebobbibobbi

beebeebobbi

beebeebobbibobbi

beebeebobbi

beebeebobbibobbi

beebeebobbi

beebeebobbibobbi ...." *all night long.*

The sun rose in the morning on a very tired zoo.
"What can be the matter?" said the keeper.
"The animals must be sick. The elephant is still lying down,
the lion is standing on his head, the monkeys won't swing by
their tails. Oh, dear me." And he hurried away.

"beebeebobbibobbi," said the beebee bird cheerfully,
and he settled down for his morning nap.
The lion whispered to the bear, and the bear nodded
to the others. The beebee bird was at last asleep.
"BEEBEEBOBBI," roared the lion.
"BEEBEEBOBBI," trumpeted the elephant.
"BEEBEEBOBBI," growled the bear.
"BEEBEEBOBBIBOBBI!!!" sang all the animals together.

"Quiet," said the beebee bird.
"Can't you see that I'm sleeping?
It's time for my nap."
"BEEBEEBOBBIBOBBI BEEBEEBOBBIBOBBI!!!" they roared.
The keeper came running with his arms in the air.
"SOMETHING IS WRONG!" he said. "SOMETHING
IS VERY WRONG WITH THE ANIMALS!
WHATEVER SHALL I DO?"
And he jumped up and down with alarm.

"BEEBEEBOBBI!!!" sang the animals
all
day
long. . . .

And the baby beebee bird simply couldn't
sleep at all.

— The sun went down and the moon came up —

"Beebeebobbi," whispered the lion, who was too tired to roar.
"Bobbibeebee," sighed the elephant as he closed his eyes.
"Bee . . . . . bee . . . . bob . . . bi . . . ." said a
monkey, half to himself.

And then . . .

all was still.

The moon shone down upon a sleeping zoo.
Not an ear or a tail or a whisker moved,
and high, high up in the linden tree
a tiny bird, inside a leaf,
was fast asleep.

And now everyday at the zoo you can hear
"beebeebobbibobbi beebeebobbibobbi" in between the lion's roars,
but at night there is never a sound.
Nighttime is really best for sleeping...
especially for very little birds.